sleepy solar system

By Dr. John Hutton

Illustrated by Doug Cenko

Published by blue manatee press,
Cincinnati, Ohio.
blue manatee press and associated logo
are registered trademarks of Arete Ventures, LLC.

First Edition: Fall, 2016.

Library of Congress Cataloging-In-Publication Data
Sleepy Solar System / by John S. Hutton: illustrated by Doug Cenko—1st ed.
Summary: Join the planets (and a few friends) as they settle into bedtime routines, such as
washing dusty faces, brushing rings, and asking for one more hug and kiss. Rhyming text and whimsical
illustrations provide an enchanting read-aloud and a celebration of the wonders of outer space,
including a map and facts at the end.
ISBN-13 (hardcover): 978-1-936669-49-3
[Juvenile Fiction - Bedtime & Dreams. 2. Juvenile Fiction - Science & Technology.]
Printed in the USA.

To Sandy and our daughters—
my sun, moon, and stars.

-JH

For Janna and Olive—
my two favorite people on Earth.

-DC

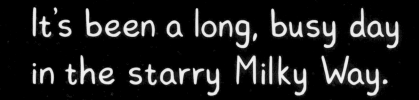

It's been a long, busy day
in the starry Milky Way.

Sleepy, setting Sun calls out,
"Bedtime, everyone."

Dizzy Mercury says, "At last—
been spinning so fast."

Sister Venus with a yawn,
puts a cozy nightgown on.

Mother Earth is sleepy too,
in pajamas green and blue.

Grumpy Mars washes red
from his rusty, dusty head.

Jupiter scrubs a stormy spot
with a washcloth—
cool, not hot.

Saturn brushes rainbow rings
with a bubbly toothbrush thing.

A bedtime story from Uranus
is sure to entertain us,

as asteroids zoom and fly
across the twinkling sky.

Neptune pulls a snuggly sheet over icy, chilly feet.

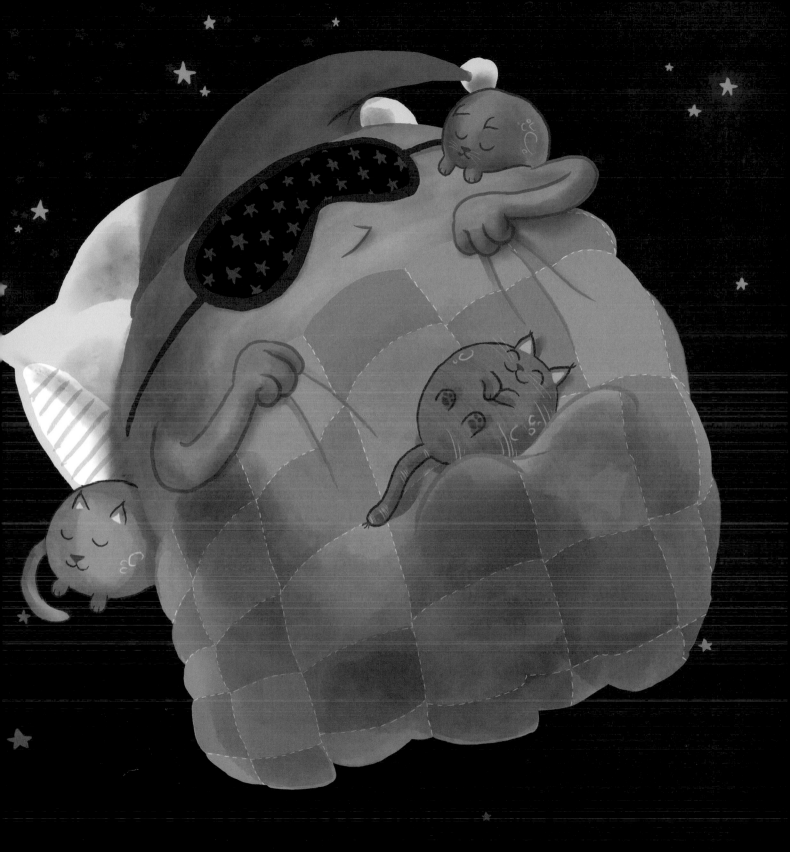

Teeny Pluto (not to miss)
asks for one more hug and kiss.

And as mellow Father Moon
turns on a pale night light...

Together, the planets whisper,
"Sweet dreams, goodnight."

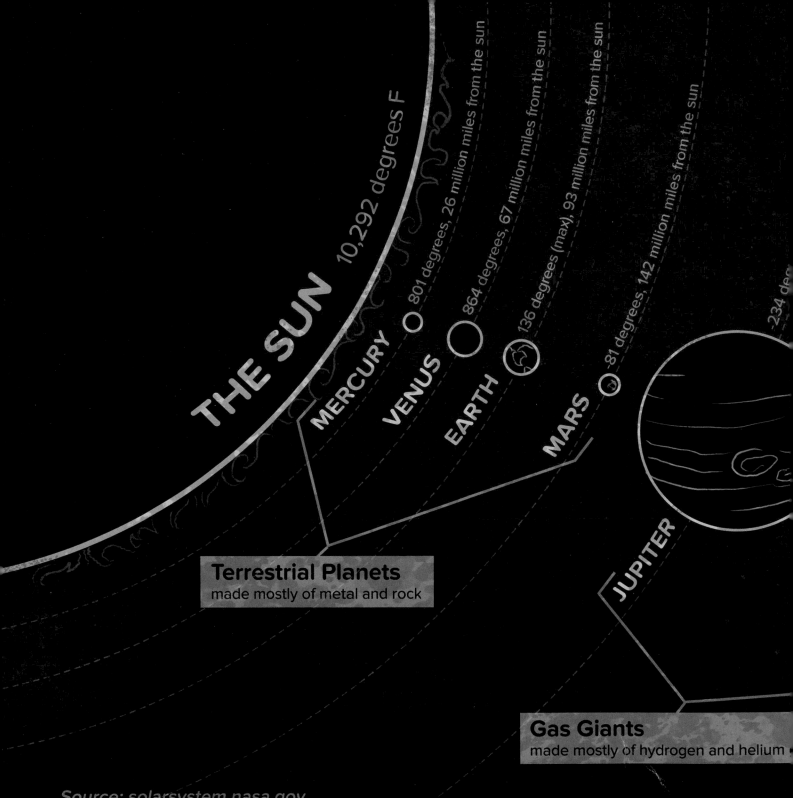

THE SUN 10,292 degrees F

MERCURY ○ 801 degrees, 26 million miles from the sun

VENUS ○ 864 degrees, 67 million miles from the sun

EARTH ◉ 136 degrees (max), 93 million miles from the sun

MARS ◉ -81 degrees, 142 million miles from the sun

-234 deg

JUPITER

Terrestrial Planets
made mostly of metal and rock

Gas Giants
made mostly of hydrogen and helium

Source: solarsystem.nasa.gov

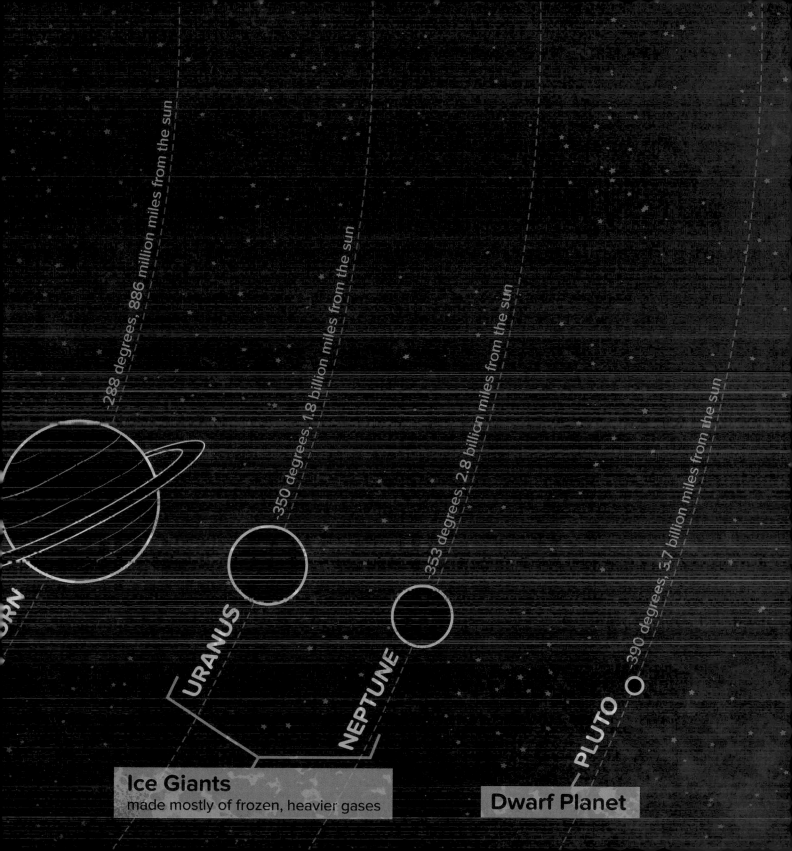

-288 degrees, 886 million miles from the sun

-350 degrees, 1.8 billion miles from the sun

-353 degrees, 2.8 billion miles from the sun

-390 degrees, 3.7 billion miles from the sun

URN

URANUS

NEPTUNE

PLUTO

Ice Giants
made mostly of frozen, heavier gases

Dwarf Planet

★ The sun is a **star**—the closest star to the Earth. It is made of burning gas.

★ Mercury is a **fast** planet. It zooms around the sun at an average of 107 thousand miles per hour!

★ Venus is a **bright** planet. It's hot, too—864 degrees Fahrenheit! On Earth, you can see it in the sky at night.

★ Earth is a **lively** planet, and also a wet one. Most of the Earth's surface is covered in water.

✦ Mars is a **rusty** planet. Its soil rusts, giving the ground there a red color; that's why Mars's nickname is the **Red Planet**.

★ Jupiter is a **stormy** planet. Jupiter's **Great Red Spot** is a gigantic storm (about the size of Earth) that has been raging for hundreds of years!

Know?

Saturn is a **ringed** planet. Its lovely rings are made of billions of small chunks of ice and rock.

Uranus is a **tilted** planet. It spins on its side, due to a crash with another planet long ago. It was also the first planet to be discovered with a telescope.

Neptune is a **windy** planet. On Neptune, the wind can blow at more than 1,200 miles per hour!

Pluto is a **tiny** planet (also called a dwarf planet), smaller than our Moon. It's also the coldest planet— -380 degrees Fahrenheit!

The moon is not a planet, but it is the only other place in the solar system that humans have **visited**.

Asteroids are **rocky** and very far apart from each other—usually more than 1.2 million miles apart!

Source: solarsystem.nasa.gov